STAR WARS®

THE CLONE WARS™

Jar Jar's Big Day

Adapted by Rob Valois

Grosset & Dunlap • LucasBooks

GROSSET & DUNLAP
Published by the Penguin Group
Penguin Group (USA) Inc., 375 Hudson Street, New York, New York 10014, USA
Penguin Group (Canada), 90 Eglinton Avenue East, Suite 700,
Toronto, Ontario M4P 2Y3, Canada
(a division of Pearson Penguin Canada Inc.)
Penguin Books Ltd., 80 Strand, London WC2R 0RL, England
Penguin Group Ireland, 25 St. Stephen's Green, Dublin 2, Ireland
(a division of Penguin Books Ltd.)
Penguin Group (Australia), 250 Camberwell Road, Camberwell, Victoria 3124, Australia
(a division of Pearson Australia Group Pty. Ltd.)
Penguin Books India Pvt. Ltd., 11 Community Centre,
Panchsheel Park, New Delhi—110 017, India
Penguin Group (NZ), 67 Apollo Drive, Rosedale, North Shore 0632, New Zealand
(a division of Pearson New Zealand Ltd.)
Penguin Books (South Africa) (Pty.) Ltd., 24 Sturdee Avenue,
Rosebank, Johannesburg 2196, South Africa

Penguin Books Ltd., Registered Offices:
80 Strand, London WC2R 0RL, England

This book is published in partnership with LucasBooks, a division of Lucasfilm Ltd.

ISBN 978-0-448-45223-4   10 9 8 7 6 5 4 3 2 1

WHO'S WHO

Battle droids: The robotic army of the Separatist Alliance.

C-3PO: Padmé's protocol droid. He hates adventure and space travel.

Chancellor Palpatine: Leader of the Galactic Republic.

Clone troopers: Identical soldiers who protect the Republic.

Jar Jar Binks: A junior representative in the Galactic Senate. He is very clumsy and often gets himself into a lot of trouble.

Nute Gunray: Head of the Trade Federation and a high-ranking member of the Separatist Alliance, the enemy of the Republic.

Padmé Amidala: Senator of the Galactic Republic.

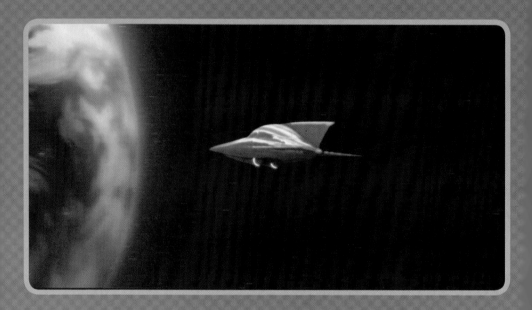

Senator Padmé Amidala, C-3PO, and Jar Jar Binks were on an important mission. The Senator from the planet of Rodia had asked to meet with Padmé. He needed the Republic's help in the war against the Separatist Alliance.

Padmé and C-3PO listened to a holographic message from Chancellor Palpatine.

Jar Jar wanted to see what was happening.

But C-3PO was always in the way.

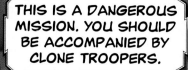

THIS IS A DANGEROUS MISSION. YOU SHOULD BE ACCOMPANIED BY CLONE TROOPERS.

YOUSA NO NEEDIN' TO WORRY, I CAN HELP . . .

Jar Jar accidentally hit the ship's controls.

And it rocked back and forth.

JAR JAR, LOOK OUT!

WONK

Jar Jar stumbled and knocked C-3PO to the ground.

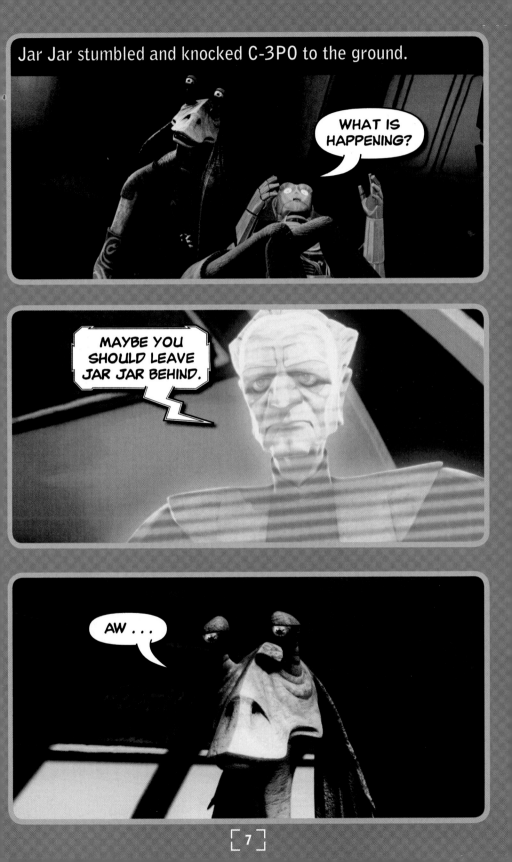

WHAT IS HAPPENING?

MAYBE YOU SHOULD LEAVE JAR JAR BEHIND.

AW . . .

The ship landed on the planet's surface.

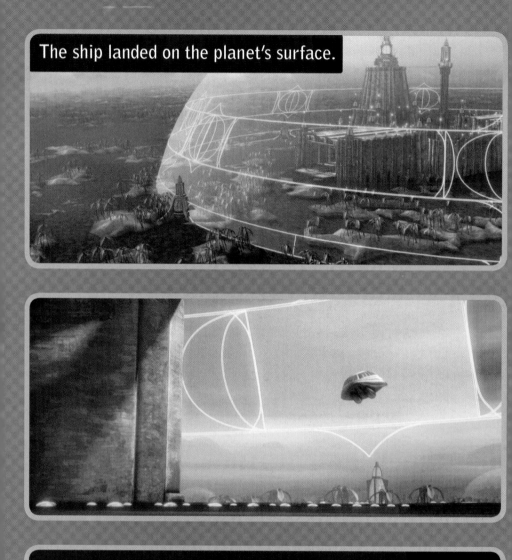

And Padmé left for the mission without Jar Jar or C-3PO.

Jar Jar and C-3PO waited for Padmé to return.

But then they heard something coming.

CLANK CLANK

OH MY STARS, BATTLE DROIDS!

WEESA IN TROUBLE NOW!

Jar Jar ran back to the ship. C-3PO was left behind.

WAIT FOR ME!

Jar Jar reached out to help C-3PO into the ship.

But C-3PO was too heavy.

And Jar Jar fell out of the ship.

JAR JAR, YOU GREAT WEBFOOT! YOU ARE SQUASHING MY CIRCUITS!

Jar Jar ran off and left C-3PO on the ground.

But he tripped over the power controls for a giant magnet.

The magnet swung around and stopped right over C-3PO.

Jar Jar found something interesting inside their destroyed ship.

Jar Jar put on the Jedi robe as a disguise.

Out on the landing platform, they saw a ship arriving.

It was the evil Nute Gunray.

WHERE IS PADMÉ AMIDALA?

WE ARE HOLDING HER IN THE DETENTION TOWER.

Padmé had been taken prisoner by the Separatists!

WEESA GOTTA RESCUE'N HER!

LOOK! A JEDI!

The battle droid thought that Jar Jar was a Jedi.

MEESA NOT A JEDI!

STOP HIM!

But before the droids could get to him, Jar Jar climbed through a grate on the ground.

And he fell into the swampy water below.

Luckily, Jar Jar could breathe underwater.

But there was a giant swamp monster down there.

DERSA BAD BOOGIE MONSTER DOWN HERE, YOU BETCHA.

And Jar Jar swam off as fast as he could.

Use these stickers with the poster at the back of the book.

Jar Jar climbed back onto the surface. Everyone was gone.

He had to rescue Padmé.

So he climbed up the tower.

Jar Jar finally made it to the top of the tower.

He could hear Nute Gunray and a droid talking.

BRING ME PADMÉ AMIDALA.

SHE ESCAPED.

ESCAPED!

But Jar Jar jumped through a grate and dove back into the water . . .

. . . where he ran into the swamp monster again.

WHAAAAH!

Jar Jar swam off, but the swamp monster followed him.

C-3PO was captured by droids.

YOU'RE UNDER ARREST.

OH DEAR.

And he was held prisoner along with Padmé who had been captured again.

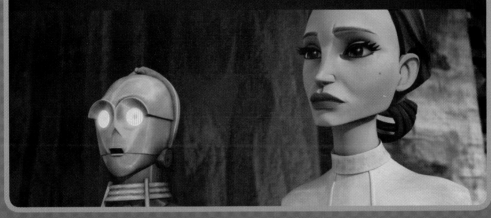

Jar Jar climbed out of the swamp to help his friends.

IT'S THE JEDI!

Everyone turned to see Jar Jar standing behind them.

Jar Jar pretended that he really was a Jedi.

All the droids turned and pointed their blasters at Jar Jar.

Before the droids could do anything, the swamp monster burst up through the grate and Jar Jar was thrown up onto its back.

THE JEDI HAS SUMMONED A MONSTER!

The droids began firing at the monster as Gunray fled to his escape ship.

Jar Jar tried his best to hold on to his new friend.

The swamp monster raised its head up and knocked Jar Jar to the ground.

OUCH!

Then it swung its tail and knocked Gunray's ship into the swamp.

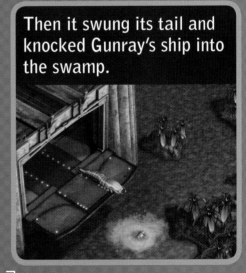

HOLD IT RIGHT THERE, GUNRAY.

Nute Gunray turned to run, but Jedi Jar Jar blocked his way.

YOU ARE GOING TO SPEND THE REST OF THE WAR IN A CELL.

They heard the sound of ships overhead.

THOSE ARE REPUBLIC SHIPS! THE CLONE TROOPERS HAVE ARRIVED!

The clone troopers surrounded Nute Gunray.

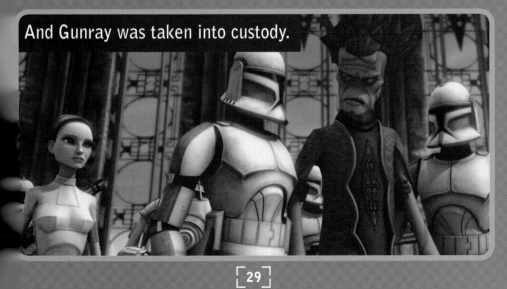

And Gunray was taken into custody.

The clone commander saluted Jar Jar.

WHAT ARE YOUR ORDERS, GENERAL?

He thought that Jar Jar was a real Jedi.

C-3PO couldn't believe that anyone could think Jar Jar was a Jedi.

With their mission over, they received another holographic message from Chancellor Palpatine.

THE CAPTURE OF GUNRAY WAS A MAJOR VICTORY FOR THE REPUBLIC.

ALL OF YOU SHOULD BE COMMENDED FOR YOUR COURAGE.

ESPECIALLY YOU, JAR JAR BINKS.

Jar Jar stood proudly next to Padmé and C-3PO. He might not have been a real Jedi, but he definitely was a hero.